It's A Sunny Life

by Gary Lezak

illustrated by Rob Peters

Special Thanks To:

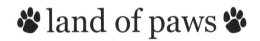

It's A Sunny Life

by Gary Lezak
illustrated by Rob Peters

www.ascendbooks.com

Requests for permission should be addressed to: Ascend Books, LLC, Attn: Rights and Permissions Department, 12710 Pflumm Road, Suite 200, Olathe, KS 66062

10 9 8 7 6 5 4 3 2 1

ISBN: print book 978-0-9966742-3-2
ISBN: e-book 978-0-9966742-4-9
Library of Congress Control Number: 2016907021

Publisher: Bob Snodgrass
Editors: Aaron Cedeño and Teresa Sosinski
Publication Coordinator: Christine Drummond
Sales and Marketing: Lenny Cohen
Dust Jacket, Book Design, and Illustrations: Rob Peters

The goal of Ascend Books is to publish quality works. With that goal in mind, we are proud to offer this book to our readers. Please notify the publisher of any erroneous credits or omissions, and corrections will be made to subsequent editions/future printings. Please note, however, that the story, experiences, and the words are those of the author alone.

Printed in Canada

www.ascendbooks.com

Dedications

I would like to dedicate this book to all pet owners, especially the ones who adopt dogs and cats from animal shelters. I now adopt all of my dogs from area shelters.

I also want to dedicate this book to the television stations and broadcast companies I have worked for. Scripps Howard Broadcasting and KSHB-TV have allowed me to share my dogs on television with the viewing audience since 1999. My weather dogs have been on television every week for over 25 years, beginning with Windy The Weather Dog on KWTV-TV in Oklahoma City in the early 1990s.

Contents

Meet Windy, Breezy, and Stormy! They belong to Gary, a cool TV weather man who has been making people smile with stories about his dogs for more than 20 years.

Stormy

One day, the three dogs were snuggling on the couch, watching Gary on TV. After the weather forecast he began talking about a new puppy he was going to adopt.

"A new puppy?" they thought.
"Why didn't we know about this?"

"What do you think he will name her?"
Windy asked her doggy sisters.

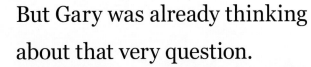

But Gary was already thinking about that very question.

In fact, right at that moment, he asked the TV viewers what name *they* would choose. There were so many possibilities: Misty, Hailey, Rainy, Foggy, and many more!

Finally Gary decided, "Sunny" would be the new dog's name!

When he got home they all jumped in the car and went to the animal shelter to pick her up.

Sunny was so excited to be part
of a new family!

Gary could tell Windy,
Breezy, and Stormy were a
little uneasy about adding
to their family. An idea
came to him.

"I know!" he said. "We need to spend some time together and get to know each other... Let's go on an adventure!"

Windy, Breezy, and Stormy heard this and their ears perked up. An adventure meant a car ride, and they did love car rides. So they thought, "Why not? Let's go!"

Sunny was still very young and car rides made her nervous.

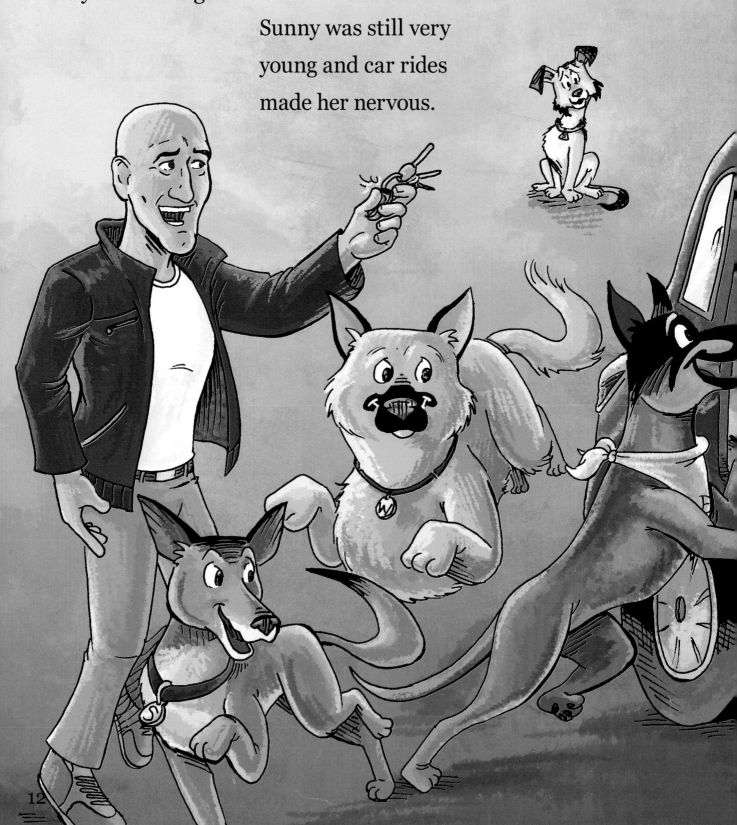

Her sisters did their best to make her feel comfortable. They all laid down in the back of the car to show her what to do.

Once everyone was settled, off they went!

During the trip, Windy, Breezy, and Stormy sometimes stuck their heads out the open windows of the car. They loved the way the wind caught their ears and caused them to flap and flutter.

Sunny still wasn't so sure. She hadn't been on many car rides before, let alone on an adventure like this one. But the other dogs encouraged her. It was so exciting to hear all the new sounds, smell all the new smells, and see all the new sights!

The car slowed down. Windy, Breezy, and Stormy perked up. They knew what that meant. When the car finally stopped and Gary opened the doors, that's when the adventure would really begin!

Sunny wanted to join in the excitement, but she couldn't help being a little scared. This was just all so new to her. Even so, she jumped out of the car to follow Gary and her sisters.

Gary explained they had arrived at the Rocky Mountains in Colorado, and that they were going to go hiking and exploring together. On went their leashes and off they went, to hear, see, and smell everything the mountains had to offer.

Along the way they played in mountain streams and sniffed the beautiful flowers. There was so much to see and do!

In the sky, the clouds began to grow thick and dark. Gary knew a big thunderstorm was brewing.

It was time to head back to the car.

BOOM!

Lightning flashed
and a clap of
thunder followed.

Sunny was very scared! She
panicked, and accidentally
slipped off her new collar.

With no leash holding her, she ran as fast as she could to get away from the terrifying noise. Gary called out for her but Sunny was already too far away to hear.

Sunny ran and ran. Just as the rain began to fall in big, fat drops, she spotted a little cave. She dashed inside to get out of the storm.

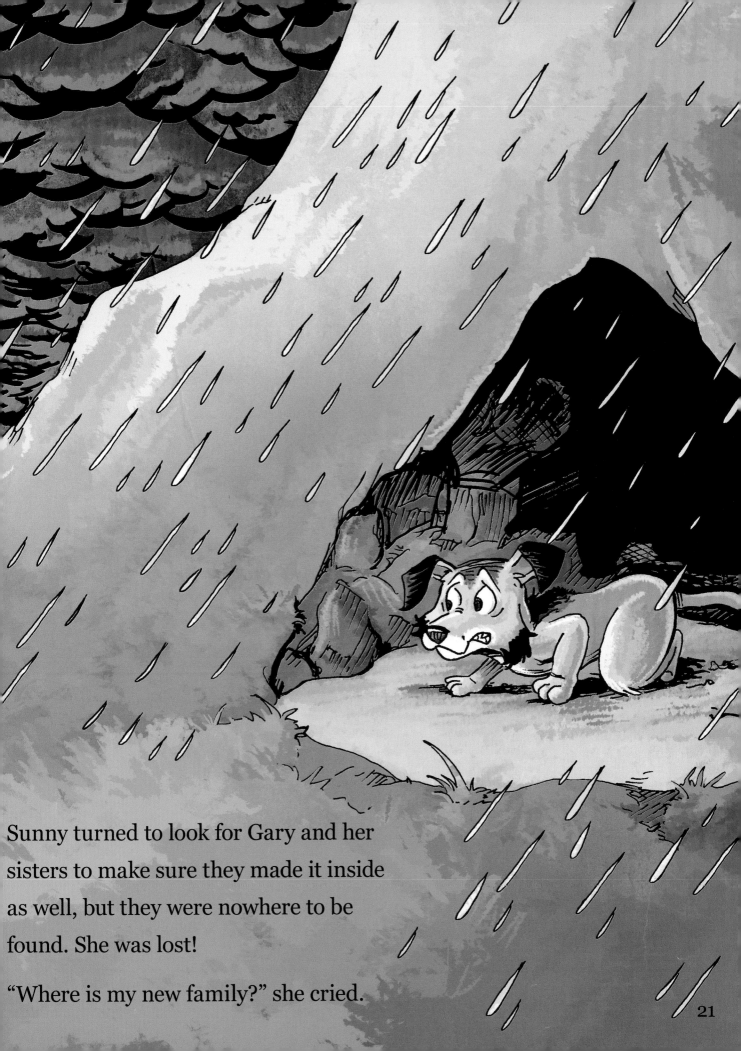

Sunny turned to look for Gary and her sisters to make sure they made it inside as well, but they were nowhere to be found. She was lost!

"Where is my new family?" she cried.

Because of how high up the mountain Sunny had run, the rain soon turned to snow. She was cold and wet. She wished she had never even gotten out of the car. Then she heard a friendly voice behind her.

"Excuse me," the voice said. "My name is Jamie. Have you lost your family?"

Sunny jumped and quickly turned to see who was talking. It was another dog! A boy, named Jamie. It made Sunny feel so much better to know that she was not alone.

22

The snow finally stopped falling, leaving a thick white blanket on the ground. Jamie nudged Sunny toward the cave's entrance.

"I've been on many adventures, and have even been as scared as you are now!" he said. "I know what to do. Go run around in the snow. Your paw prints will help your family find you. But don't go too far!"

Sunny had never felt snow, but once she did she
found out she loved it! She ran and ran, stopping to
roll and play, and make plenty of paw prints for her
family to find.

After a while, Sunny returned to the cave and ran to Jamie.

"I made so many paw prints," she said, excitedly. "They are sure to find me!"

Sunny was so tired and laid down next to Jamie. As her eyes began to close, she listened to Jamie telling her a story about how much her family loved her and that they would find her.

Meanwhile, lower on the mountain, the rain had stopped but lightning and dark clouds still filled the sky. Gary, Windy, Breezy, and Stormy sat in the car, waiting for the storm to pass.

"Once this clears up, we'll head out and find Sunny," Gary told them.

As soon as the dark clouds blew away, Gary, Windy, Stormy, and Breezy set out to find Sunny. They walked up the mountain and saw the ground was covered with sparkling white snow.

Everyone called out for Sunny, barking and yelling her name as loudly as they could.

The higher they climbed, the more snow had fallen. Soon, Windy noticed a trail of paw prints. She barked to get the attention of the others and trotted off toward the prints.

Could this be a clue from Sunny? Gary wondered. "Let's follow these paw prints and see where they take us," Gary said.

After a while the paw prints came
to a stop in front of a small cave.
And inside...

"SUNNY!" they all exclaimed.
She ran out to them, her tail
wagging as fast as it would go.

Sunny tackled Gary to the ground and was joined
by her sisters. They covered him and each other in
wet doggy kisses.

Gary laughed and got to his feet. Breezy asked, "Sunny, how did you know to leave paw prints for us?"

Sunny smiled. "Jamie told me."

The other three dogs looked at her in surprise. "Jamie?" Stormy asked. "We had a brother named Jamie a long time ago."

"Come on!" Sunny said as she danced back and forth between her family and the cave. "I'll show you!"

Jamie wasn't there and Sunny
didn't understand.

"Jamie was here," Sunny insisted.
"But now he is gone."

Gary quickly got everyone's attention. "Come on!" he called out. "I've got something special to show you!"

Instead of going back down the mountain, he led them on the snow-covered trail up to the mountain top.

After a long hike they arrived at the top. It was a difficult climb that left them all panting. Even Gary looked tired.

As they looked up, they saw that their effort had been worth it. The view was unlike anything they had ever seen. The setting sun was shining on the snow and they could see for miles.

Sunny admired the beauty all around her,
and then looked at her wonderful new family.
"Now I know," she said. "I will definitely have a
'sunny' life."

Sunny's Weather Academy

Welcome, Junior Meteorologists, to **Sunny's Weather Academy!** Here is where you can learn more about the weather to prepare you and your family for what nature may have in store for you.

Knowing about the weather is important for many reasons. Should you wear shorts or jeans today? Can you play outside? What should you do if a thunderstorm is coming, or during a tornado warning, to stay safe and sound? Sunny knows! She's learned from Gary, and now she wants to teach you! So put on your thinking cap and follow along!

We will begin with the first thing you should learn about weather. It is Gary's favorite weather topic: clouds. And, then we will learn about precipitation coming out of the clouds, and, what happens when cloud formations turn into storms. Finally, we learn what to do when a threatening storm approaches or you find yourself in a storm.

The Ten Types of Clouds

I already know what you're thinking. Ten types of clouds are a lot of clouds, especially when you look up into the sky and it seems you are still seeing the same white, fluffy shapes you always do. But look a little closer, and you'll see the differences – important differences! Here are the main types of clouds.

1. **Cirrus** – These are clouds that form around 20,000 feet up above us. They look very delicate and wispy, almost as if they'd break apart if you could wave your hand through them. They are always made of ice crystals, and are the first to light up with the sunrise and last to go out with the sunset.

2. **Cirrostratus** – These are also very thin, but usually grouped together in a sheet covering the entire sky. They are so thin that when the sun or moon shines through them, it appears to create a "halo" effect as the light bounces through the ice crystals in the cloud.

3. **Cirrocumulus** – Small, "puffball" clouds that typically appear in rows, and are either white or gray. Cirrocumulus clouds are in the high cloud "Cirrus Family" of clouds that also form 20,000 feet above us.

4. **Altocumulus** – These clouds form a little lower in the sky than the Cirrus clouds. Altocumuluses usually clump together in groups, and if you see them on a particularly humid morning, they can be a sign of an afternoon thunderstorm.

5. **Altostratus** – Another type of "mid-level" cloud, altostratus are typically more gray than white in color, and blanket the sky in a thin layer. Sunshine can peek through them, but it will appear to be hazy or fuzzy. If you see these, a longer-lasting rain or snowstorm could be one day away.

6. **Nimbostratus** – These low clouds are thick and dark and cover the entire sky. Nimbus means rain, and this is one of the main types of clouds that produces rain and snow. Nimbostratus form in a dark, gray layer thick enough to blot out the sun.

7. **Stratus** – Forming very low to the ground, these clouds are gray through and through and will cover most or all of the sky. Stratus clouds can look like fog that doesn't quite touch the ground, and can produce mist or drizzle. When it is foggy, this means the stratus cloud is on the ground.

8. **Cumulus** – These clouds start low but grow high in the sky. They have a broad, flat base and fluffy tops, look like giant cotton balls, and are typically white or light gray.

9. **Stratocumulus** – Another low-building cloud, stratocumulus clouds are lumpy and gray in appearance. You won't get a heavy rain from these, but they will drizzle. Most of the time they can be found in rows, although they will spread out from time to time.

10. **Cumulonimbus** – Whoa, that name is a mouthful. It's maybe easier to just call them "thunderstorm clouds." Much like cumulus clouds, these will start lower in the atmosphere but can grow to incredible heights. Because they grow so tall, the typically fluffy head characteristic of a cumulus cloud is flattened out and turns into ice crystals spreading out into the shape of an anvil on the top of the cloud. They are associated with heavy rain, snow, hail, lightning, and even tornadoes. The cumulonimbus cloud is the thunderhead, and can grow from a base of 3,000 feet or lower all the way up to 70,000 feet above the surface in the largest thunderstorms.

Let's summarize. Look at the illustration above to see the ten basic types of clouds.

- **Low clouds:** Stratus, Stratocumulus, and Nimbostratus
- **Middle clouds:** Altostratus and Altocumulus
- **High clouds:** Cirrus, Cirrostratus, and Cirrocumulus
- **Clouds that can grow from low to high:** Cumulonimbus, Cumulus

The low clouds will form below 5,000 feet. The middle clouds will form from 5,000 feet to 15,000 feet above the ground. And, the high clouds form closer to 20,000 feet above us.

Use this cloud chart to figure out which type of cloud you are seeing. When a storm is approaching, you can use the cloud types to help forecast the weather. The first clouds you may see will be the high clouds, cirrus, cirrostratus, or cirrocumulus. As a storm gets closer they will likely lower in to the middle clouds of altostratus and altocumulus. And, then as the storm begins to produce precipitation they will become nimbostratus or cumulonimbus. If it is raining or snowing, then it will be a nimbostratus or cumulonimbus cloud.

What is Precipitation?

Precipitation: When water, in any form, falls from the clouds it is called precipitation.

If you watch Gary on TV or follow his blog, you'll hear this word a lot: Precipitation. But what is it? In simple terms, it can be any kind of liquid or solid water particle that falls from the sky and reaches the ground.

The process of creating precipitation begins when a mass of warm, moist air runs into a mass of cold air. The condensation that is created forms droplets that either harden into ice crystals or become rain. And when they get too heavy, those droplets are what fall to Earth.

There are different types of precipitation that fall from the biggest clouds. Here are the main precipitation types:

- **Rain**
- **Snow**
- **Hail**
- **Sleet**
- **Freezing Rain**
- **Graupel**

(You can learn more about these types of precipitation in the Sunny's Weather Words section.)

Sleet is actually rain that is falling and it freezes on the way down to the ground. The raindrops freeze into small pieces of ice.

Hail will also start as a raindrop freezing into a small piece of ice, but it is turbulent inside thunderstorms where hail forms. Hail can grow in this turbulent motion and become quite large, even as big as softballs or larger, and this can become life threatening.

Freezing rain is different than sleet. Freezing rain is in liquid form as rain drops until it reaches the surface and freezes on contact. If the temperature is below freezing near the ground the rain drops will freeze on trees, powerlines, cars, and roads and can cause all kinds of problems. It is rare, but when it gets bad it will be called an ice storm.

Graupel is a type of precipitation in the form of snow pellets or soft hail. It can happen just about anywhere winter types of precipitation fall, but occurs most often over mountainous areas like the Rocky Mountains.

Types of Storms

An atmospheric storm system is a disturbance that causes rain, snow, sleet, hail, lightning, thunder, or just wind. Storms come in different sizes and strength.

A **hurricane** is a type of storm system that forms over warm tropical waters and is usually hundreds of miles across.

Though small in size, the strongest storm on earth is the **tornado**, and this is usually only around one-tenth of a mile wide on average, but can grow to larger than one mile in the strongest and worst tornadoes. Winds inside tornadoes can reach speeds of over 300 miles per hour.

Thunderstorms are a type of storm system that is about five to ten miles across. There is a way to determine if the thunderstorm is moving towards you or moving away from you. Remember when lightning flashes, you see it almost instantly as the speed of light is 186,000 miles per second. But sound travels slower than light; it travels about one mile in five seconds. So, the first time you see lightning, start counting the seconds until you hear the sound of thunder. If it's ten seconds, then you know the thunderstorm is two miles away. (Remember that sound travels at the speed of one mile in five seconds.) The next time you see lightning, start counting the seconds again and stop counting when you hear the thunder. Was it less time? Then you know the storm is moving closer to you. If it was a longer time, then the storm is moving away from you.

Severe Weather & Severe Weather Safety

Severe weather can come in the form of a hurricane, tornado, damaging wind, large hail, dust storm, blizzard, ice storm and more. The most immediate dangers with severe weather comes when we have thunderstorms that get too strong. When a thunderstorm becomes severe you should take cover immediately.

A severe weather **watch** means conditions are favorable for the kind of weather issued in the watch.

A severe weather **warning** means that you may be in immediate danger and you should take action now.

When a Tornado Warning is issued:

- You should take action when a tornado warning is issued and you hear the warning sirens in your neighborhood.
- Go to the lowest level of a building or home or the smallest room preferably in the middle of the house or building. If there is a basement, go there.
- Don't worry about your windows. If they are open, leave them open. If they are closed, leave them closed.
- You should stay in this safe place until you hear the "all clear signal" from your television or radio.

When a Flash Flood Warning is issued:

- If you are in a car, don't drive toward or through the water – turn around and go to higher ground. Do not try to drive across a road that has water flowing across it. It only takes about one foot of water to cause your car to float away.
- During a Flash Flood Warning stay indoors. Do not play near creeks or rivers.

Sunny's list of supplies just in case severe weather threatens. Place the items below in waterproof bags or containers

- First aid kit
- Bottled water
- Weather radio
- Extra batteries
- Blankets and sleeping bags
- Food/protein bars
- Flashlight
- Whistle
- Duct tape
- Candles
- Shoes
- Car keys
- Cell phone charger

Supplies for Pets

- Recent photos of your pets, in case they get lost
- Pet first aid kit
- 3 to 7 days-worth of dry food
- Bottled water
- Crate or carrier
- Collar, leash, and toys
- Pet feeding dishes
- Disposable litter trays and cat litter
- Garbage bags for clean-up

Now that you have learned the weather basics, Gary and Sunny The Weather Dog would love for you to join **Sunny's Weather Academy.** Find out more at www.ascendbooks.com and www.Weather2020.com

Sunny's Weather Words

When you watch Gary on TV, you probably hear some words that are new and unfamiliar. Have you ever wondered what a barometer is? Or a meteorologist? Or precipitation?

It can be a little confusing. To help, here are some of the most common weather-words you will need to know. Also included is what each word means.

Arctic Air – Air that moves south from Canada and near the North Pole, bringing us colder temperatures.

Atmosphere – An invisible mixture of gases, like oxygen, that surrounds the Earth. The air we breathe is part of the atmosphere.

Autumn – The season between summer and winter. It's also called fall!

Barometer – A tool that is used to measure the weight of the air, which is called air pressure or barometric pressure. This helps us predict changes in the weather.

Blizzard – A severe snowstorm that goes on for a long time, with winds over 35 mph reducing visibility.

Breeze – A light, gentle wind.

Cirrus cloud – A thin, wispy-looking cloud made of ice crystals that form high in the atmosphere usually around 20,000 feet above us.

Clear – When Gary is talking about the sky, "clear" means it is cloudless!

Climate – The general weather conditions over a longer period of time. While weather can change daily, climate changes over much longer periods.

Cold Front – An imaginary line between two large air masses, one colder and one warmer. When a cold front passes, the colder air replaces the warmer air.

Cumulus cloud– A type of cloud that is thick and fluffy, with a round top and a flat bottom. Sometimes cumulus clouds will look like animals or other things in the sky.

Dew – Water that forms on the ground during a clear, calm night, when the air becomes so cool that it needs to release moisture.

Earth – The third planet from the sun and it's where we live.

El Niño – What weather experts call the warming of the surface of the eastern tropical Pacific Ocean. When this happens, it affects wind patterns that can then change weather in many places on Earth.

Drought – A long period of time (months or years) when it rains very little.

Flood – When the land is covered by water because of heavy rain, or when a stream or river is overflowing.

Fog – A thick cloud of tiny water droplets lying on or very near the Earth's surface.

Freeze – This is when temperatures drop to 32°F (0°C) or lower. This is the temperature at which water turns from a liquid to a solid (water turns to ice)

Freezing Rain – Rain that freezes when it hits a very, very cold surface. This can happen when the temperature is above freezing high in the atmosphere but very cold near the ground.

Frost – Ice crystals that form on any surface, like leaves or grass. Frost is like dew, except it occurs when the air temperature drops near or below freezing and there is enough moisture to freeze on the grass. It can make the grass turn white.

Funnel Cloud – A visible spinning column of air, usually a lowered cloud that is in the shape of a funnel. If the circulation touches the ground, it becomes a tornado.

Graupel – A type of precipitation in the form of snow pellets or soft hail. It can happen just about anywhere winter types of precipitation fall, but occurs most often over mountainous areas.

Hail – Raindrops that freeze in the rising air inside thunderstorms. They can grow to large sizes, as large as a softball or bigger. They finally fall to the ground when they become heavy enough.

Humidity – The amount of moisture in the air.

Hurricane – A large, powerful storm that develops over warm tropical oceans. The wind needs to be at least 74 mph for the storm to be called a hurricane.

Jet Stream – A strong air current – with winds that can exceed 100 mph – high above Earth's surface where airplanes fly, around 30,000 feet above us.

Lightning – A very quick and powerful burst of electrical energy that forms between a cloud and the ground, or stays in the cloud. It usually includes a bright flash and booming thunder.

Meteorology – The study of Earth's atmosphere and all its changes. A meteorologist is someone who studies meteorology and uses it to predict the weather! Gary is a meteorologist!

Overcast – When a layer of clouds covers the entire sky.

Precipitation – Any type of water that falls to the ground from the sky. It can be rain, snow, sleet, freezing rain, or hail!

Rain – Water droplets that fall to Earth. Rain forms inside a cloud as water vapor collects around tiny bits of dust or salt to make larger and larger droplets.

Rain Gauge – An instrument used to measure how much rain has fallen during a period of time.

Rainbow – A rainbow is caused by sunlight reflecting off the back of water droplets in the air. As the sunlight bounces back toward us from different directions, it forms an arcing bow of beautiful colors. When you see a rainbow, the sun will always be behind you!

Sleet – A type of precipitation that takes the shape of ice pellets. It's usually mixed with rain or snow.

Snow – Ice crystals that combine together, and grow. These form inside cold clouds during the winter. They will grow and then fall to the earth as beautiful flakes.

Snow Flurries – When snow falls for a very brief period, and produces very little or no accumulation.

Spring – The season between winter and summer.

Stratus Clouds – Gray, sheet-like clouds. They may be able to produce some very light mist or drizzle, but usually the weather is dry.

Summer – The season between spring and fall.

Sun – The star at the center of our solar system, and the most important source of energy for life on Earth.

Supercell – A very large, long-lasting thunderstorm that can produce large hail and tornadoes.

Thunder – A loud rumbling noise produced because lightning heats the air around it so quickly. Thunder travels about one mile every five seconds.

Thunderstorm – A storm that is produced by a cumulonimbus cloud and is always accompanied by lightning and thunder. Different types of precipitation and high winds may also occur.

Tornado – A violently spinning column of air that extends to the ground from a thunderstorm.

Visibility – How far a person can see. This is important when discussing fog, because fog limits visibility. When it's very foggy, the visibility can be near zero.

Warm Front – The opposite of a cold front! A boundary line between two air masses of different temperature, where the warmer air is replacing the colder air.

Wind – Air in motion. It is produced by the sun heating the earth's surface unevenly. Warm air rises, and cold air moves in to replace it – which is what can cause the wind to blow.

Wind Chill – A number that tells us how cold it feels to our body due to the wind's effect on the temperature.

Winter – The season between fall and spring.

Acknowledgements

I would like to thank Andy Caraway who helped write this story. Since he has been a part of the dogs' lives and loves them, he was able to contribute immensely to this story.

Shirley Posladek, of AB May in Kansas City, sat next to me on a flight from Kansas City to Dallas, TX. She inspired me with the idea of making paw prints in the snow to help Sunny find her way. Thank you so much, Shirley, for this great idea!

Robert Henson helped with the weather definitions section. I am grateful for Robert taking the time to help.

Bob Snodgrass handed me his card at Royals Fanfest and asked me to contact him if I was interested in writing a book. Thank you so much for encouraging me through the process of making this book happen.

Rob Peters, the illustrator, did a great job of capturing the dogs' personalities in the illustrations.

Thanks for sharing
our adventure.
We hope you had fun!